The Fading Echoes; The Tale of Existential Phobia

Ansh Tanwar

Published by Sellbrochure Vymish Entertainment, 2024.

THE FADING ECHOES; THE TALE OF EXISTENTIAL PHOBIA

First edition. September 11, 2024.

ISBN: 979-8227509949

Written by Ansh Tanwar.

Table of Contents

Introduction to The Fading Echoes

In the quiet corners of existence, where the boundary between reality and the ephemeral blurs, lies the heart of The Fading Echoes. This novel, an intimate tapestry woven from the threads of art, literature, and profound human experience, invites readers to journey through the landscapes of love, fear, and memory.At its core, Fading Echoes explores the existential dilemmas that haunt us all. The story follows Aarav, a reclusive artist whose life is marked by a deep-seated existential phobia. His art, once a mirror reflecting his internal anxieties, becomes a battleground where he confronts his fears of impermanence and meaninglessness. Maya, a writer with her own artistic vision, enters Aarav's world and becomes both muse and catalyst for transformation. Together, their journey becomes a quest to reconcile their inner demons with their creative expressions.

Act 1: The Spark of Connection

THE COASTAL TOWN OF Marina Cove was the kind of place that people passed through, not a place they stayed. A sleepy stretch of land, bordered by the endless blue of the ocean, it was often veiled in mist during the early mornings. The fog would settle over the town like a blanket, shrouding its weathered buildings, narrow streets, and pebble-strewn beaches in a cloak of gray. The sunsets, however, were glorious—splashes of orange and violet melting into the sea, as though the world itself was trying to prove its existence through color.

For Aarav, though, Marina Cove was not just a setting—it was a mirror of his own mind. The mist represented the confusion and fear that often settled over him, making him question his presence in the world. The sunsets, vibrant as they were, seemed more like fading moments, the last gasp of beauty before the inevitable darkness of night. Aarav had moved to the town two years ago, seeking solitude from the noise of city life. He believed that isolation might help him understand the strange sense of nothingness that haunted him, but the silence had only deepened his existential dread.

He had always been sensitive to the fleeting nature of life. Even as a child, he wondered why people lived as if they were eternal when death was certain. His art became the outlet for these thoughts, a way of confronting his own insignificance. Aarav's paintings, now stacked in the corner of his small cottage, all depicted the sea in various forms: stormy, calm, sunrise, sunset, yet always distant. The ocean, to Aarav, was the most honest representation of existence—vast, powerful, indifferent, and ultimately, empty.

Despite his growing success as an artist, Aarav never felt accomplished. Each painting, no matter how intricate, seemed to carry a hollowness, a reminder that no matter what he created, it would one day be forgotten. He lived in quiet isolation, his days marked by the rhythm of the tides and the soft hum of the wind through the trees. Friends had tried to visit, to remind him of the joys of companionship, but he had grown distant, afraid to become too close to anyone. To Aarav, forming bonds meant tethering himself to a life he was terrified would vanish without trace.

ONE MISTY AFTERNOON, Aarav walked the cobblestone streets toward the Briarwood Bookshop, a quaint little place nestled between a café and an antique store. The shop had been there for as long as he could remember, its wooden door creaking with age and the musty scent of old paper wafting from within. Books lined every wall, creating an almost labyrinthine feel inside. He often came here to browse, not out of any specific desire to read, but because the quiet atmosphere soothed his anxious thoughts.

On this particular day, as Aarav perused the philosophy section, his eyes were drawn to a woman standing by a shelf nearby. She was tall, with loose waves of dark hair cascading down her back, dressed in a light scarf and a flowy, earth-toned dress. She seemed lost in her own world, flipping through a book on existentialism with a contemplative look on her face. Something about her presence was different. She wasn't simply browsing; she was searching, as if the answers to some deep question lay between those pages. Aarav found himself unable to look away, an odd sense of connection stirring within him.

It was as if she could feel his gaze, for after a moment, she turned to him and smiled—not the polite, distant smile of a stranger, but one of recognition, as though they had met before, in another time or place.

"Are you a philosopher or an artist?" she asked suddenly, her voice soft yet tinged with curiosity.

Aarav blinked in surprise, not quite understanding the question. "Why can't I be both?" he responded, feeling slightly defensive. His paintings were, after all, his way of philosophizing, of grappling with the great unknown.

The woman's eyes sparkled with amusement as she tucked the book under her arm. "True. But most people come to philosophy either to create meaning or to search for it. Artists... they usually do the former."

Aarav considered her words. "And writers?"

She smiled. "We steal from both worlds." Extending her hand, she introduced herself. "I'm Maya, by the way."

He hesitated before shaking her hand. "Aarav."

From that moment on, Maya seemed to fill the air around them with a kind of energy that Aarav hadn't felt in a long time. She spoke with passion about the books she read, about life and death, and the thin veil that separated them. She told him that she was a writer, working on a novel that explored what it meant to exist in the shadow of nothingness. Her words resonated with him on a level he couldn't quite explain, as though she was giving voice to the fears he had been painting for years but had never articulated.

They left the bookshop together, their conversation flowing naturally as they walked along the beach. The sea, gray and restless, mirrored Aarav's inner turmoil, yet Maya seemed undeterred by the cold wind that blew in from the water. She talked about the afterlife, not with the fear or reverence most people held, but with curiosity, as if it were a distant horizon she longed to explore.

"Do you ever think about what happens when we're gone?" she asked, pausing to stare out at the ocean.

Aarav hesitated. "All the time," he admitted, his voice quieter than usual. "It's not death that scares me... it's the idea that we might just fade away, that our existence might be erased completely."

Maya nodded, her eyes thoughtful. "It's the same for me. I think that's why I write. I want to leave something behind, even if it's just words on a page."

Aarav felt a strange connection in that moment, as if Maya had somehow articulated the very essence of his phobia. They walked for hours, talking about life, art, and the fear of oblivion, until the sun began to dip below the horizon. As they watched the colors bleed into the sky, Aarav couldn't shake the feeling that Maya was different from anyone he had ever met. She wasn't afraid of the questions that haunted him; she embraced them, danced with them even.

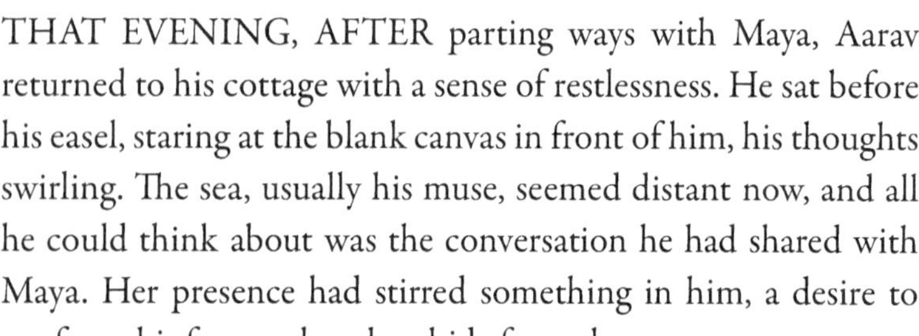

THAT EVENING, AFTER parting ways with Maya, Aarav returned to his cottage with a sense of restlessness. He sat before his easel, staring at the blank canvas in front of him, his thoughts swirling. The sea, usually his muse, seemed distant now, and all he could think about was the conversation he had shared with Maya. Her presence had stirred something in him, a desire to confront his fears rather than hide from them.

He began painting, his brush moving with purpose, but instead of the familiar waves or foggy shorelines, he painted something different: two figures standing by the sea at dusk. One figure, tall and vibrant, radiated life and energy, while the other—his own likeness—seemed to fade into the sand, his shadow growing faint against the encroaching night. The contrast was stark, almost painful, but it felt right.

As he worked, Aarav realized something: he didn't just fear fading away. He feared never truly existing in the first place.

Conclusion of Act 1:

Aarav's meeting with Maya sparks an internal shift. While his existential fears remain, Maya's vibrant presence and fearless exploration of life and death draw him out of his isolation. Their shared bond over the concept of existence creates a foundation for a deeper connection, one that challenges Aarav to confront his phobia head-on, rather than hide behind his art. The act ends with Aarav creating the first painting of Maya, a symbolic reflection of their relationship—a blend of fading echoes and vibrant life.

Act 2: The Growing Connection and Deepening Fear

THE DAYS IN MARINA Cove passed in a quiet rhythm, marked by the ebb and flow of the tide, but for Aarav, time had begun to feel different since meeting Maya. Each sunrise brought with it a renewed sense of anticipation, and each sunset seemed to pull him deeper into his own thoughts. The mundane aspects of life—his morning walks, the smell of fresh coffee from the café, even the distant cries of seagulls—had taken on a new vibrancy, as though Maya's presence had colored the world around him. Yet, with this new sense of life came a shadow, a growing fear that he couldn't shake.

As Aarav and Maya spent more time together, their bond deepened. They would often meet by the beach, their conversations ranging from the trivialities of daily life to the deepest existential questions that had always troubled Aarav. Maya seemed to exist in the world with a lightness that he envied. She wasn't weighed down by the same fears that plagued him, even though she acknowledged the uncertainties of life. For her, existence was something to explore, not to fear.

Their relationship grew organically, as though they had known each other for years. Aarav found himself opening up to Maya in ways he hadn't with anyone before. He told her about his paintings, about the way they reflected his fears of fading away, of becoming a forgotten speck in the grand scheme of the universe. Maya listened with an empathy that was both comforting and unnerving.

"Do you really think we disappear entirely when we're gone?" Maya asked one afternoon as they sat together on a weathered bench overlooking the sea. Her fingers absentmindedly traced patterns in the sand beneath her feet.

Aarav stared at the waves crashing against the rocks, feeling the weight of her question. "I don't know," he replied, his voice barely above a whisper. "I just... I can't shake the feeling that no matter what we do, it's all temporary. Our lives, our art, our memories—they're all just whispers that will eventually be drowned out."

Maya was quiet for a moment, her gaze fixed on the horizon. "But aren't those whispers enough? If someone remembers you, even for a little while, doesn't that mean you've existed in their world, even after you're gone?"

Aarav wanted to believe her, but his mind rebelled against the idea. Memories, too, were fleeting. How long before those who remembered you were gone as well? How long before your name was nothing more than a forgotten echo?

Maya sensed his hesitation and smiled softly. "I know it's hard to accept, but I think love and memories are what really keep us anchored. They're like footprints in the sand—they might fade over time, but for a while, they prove we were here."

As their relationship blossomed, Maya became Aarav's muse, in ways he hadn't expected. She would sit with him as he painted, watching as he brought the turbulent sea to life on canvas. Aarav found comfort in her presence, but at the same time, it made his fears all the more intense. The closer he grew to her, the more he feared losing her. He could see a future where Maya moved on, perhaps to another town, another life, leaving him behind. And what then? What would happen to the love they had shared? Would it vanish like the fog lifting from the shore?

One evening, Maya suggested something that both intrigued and unsettled Aarav.

"Why don't you paint your fears?" she said as they stood by his easel, her hand resting lightly on his shoulder. "You've been painting the sea for so long, but I think it's time you face what's really haunting you."

Aarav tensed, the idea swirling in his mind. He had always used his art to express the existential dread that gnawed at him, but painting his *actual fears*—the ones that kept him up at night—felt too intimate, too raw. He wasn't sure if he was ready to confront them in such a direct way.

"I don't know if I can," he admitted, his voice low. "What if putting it on canvas makes it real? What if it's something I can't take back?"

Maya's eyes softened. "Maybe that's exactly why you need to do it. Sometimes, the only way to conquer a fear is to face it head-on. If you can paint it, maybe you'll realize it's not as powerful as it seems."

Her words lingered in Aarav's mind long after she had left that evening. He stood in front of the blank canvas, his brush hovering hesitantly above the surface. For years, his paintings had been a safe space, a way to express his internal struggles without revealing too much of himself. But now, as he stared at the empty expanse before him, he felt a shift. He wasn't just painting the sea anymore. He was painting *himself*, his fear of fading, of becoming nothing more than a forgotten whisper.

The first strokes were tentative. Aarav began with the sea, as he always did, but this time, the waves were calmer, more subdued. In the center of the canvas, he painted himself, but not as a solid figure. His image was faint, almost ghostlike, his form blending with the sand beneath him. He was disappearing, piece by piece, as though the universe itself was erasing him. Standing beside him, however, was Maya, vibrant and full of life, her presence in stark contrast to his fading existence. The more he painted, the more he felt the fear gripping him—what if she would be the one to outlast him? What if, in the end, it was Maya who would be remembered, while he became nothing more than a distant memory?

THEIR CONVERSATIONS continued to circle back to this idea of existence and memory. Aarav, despite Maya's efforts, couldn't shake the growing fear that even memories were fragile, easily lost to time. He watched Maya live her life with a kind of freedom that he longed for but couldn't grasp. She wasn't afraid of what would come after; she embraced the now, the fleeting moments of joy and connection. And yet, the closer they became, the more Aarav felt trapped by his own phobia.

"You have to let go," Maya told him one night as they lay on the beach, the stars twinkling overhead. "You can't live your life in fear of what might happen. That's not living at all."

Aarav turned to her, his eyes searching hers for some kind of reassurance. "But how do you do it? How do you live without that fear?"

Maya smiled softly, reaching out to trace her fingers along his jawline. "Because I know that love and memories are enough.

I might not be here forever, but while I am, I want to leave something behind. And if someone remembers me—if *you* remember me—then that's all I need."

THE WEIGHT OF HER WORDS settled over Aarav like a blanket, comforting yet suffocating. He wanted to believe her, wanted to embrace the idea that love and memory could anchor him in the world, but the fear of losing her, and in turn losing himself, gnawed at him. Every time they touched, every time they laughed, it was bittersweet—because for every moment they shared, the clock was ticking. What if one day, she was gone? What if he was left alone, fading into nothingness, while her memory lived on?

CONCLUSION OF ACT 2:

As Aarav and Maya's relationship deepens, so too does Aarav's existential fear. Maya's belief in love and memory as anchors to existence challenges Aarav's worldview, but he struggles to embrace her perspective fully. His love for her grows, but with it, so does his fear of losing her, and consequently, his sense of self. The act ends with Aarav finishing the painting of himself disappearing into the sand, while Maya remains vibrant and full of life—an artistic reflection of his growing fear that she will outlast him in the memory of the world, while he fades away.

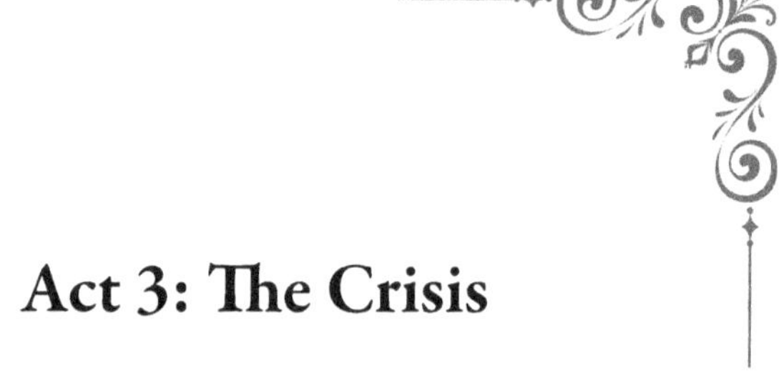

Act 3: The Crisis

THE CLOSER AARAV GOT to Maya, the more his fear of losing her—and himself—grew. For a while, he tried to ignore it, to push away the gnawing anxiety that lurked beneath the surface, but it soon became unbearable. He started to notice the small things: the way Maya's laughter seemed to linger long after she was gone, the way her scent clung to his clothes after they spent the day together, and the way her presence filled his otherwise quiet world with life. These were the very things that terrified him. How could something so beautiful be so fleeting?

As the days passed, Aarav found himself pulling away, retreating into his own mind. He stopped painting, his canvases sitting untouched in the corner of his cottage, gathering dust. The passion and drive that once fueled his art had dissipated, replaced by an overwhelming sense of dread. He couldn't bring himself to create anymore, fearing that each new painting would be a reminder of his eventual disappearance. What was the point of creating something that would one day be forgotten?

Maya noticed the change almost immediately. At first, she tried to brush it off, telling herself that Aarav was just going through one of his quieter phases, as artists often did. But as days turned into weeks, and Aarav continued to withdraw, her concern deepened. He had stopped answering her calls, avoided meeting her at their usual spots by the beach, and when they did meet, he seemed distant, as if a wall had been erected between them.

One evening, after several days of silence, Maya showed up at Aarav's cottage unannounced. She knocked on the door, her heart pounding in her chest, unsure of what to expect. When he opened the door, his face was pale, his eyes hollow, as though he hadn't slept in days.

"Aarav, what's going on?" she asked, her voice soft but tinged with frustration. "You've been avoiding me. You've stopped painting. What's happening to you?"

Aarav couldn't meet her eyes. He wanted to tell her, to explain the storm that was raging inside him, but the words caught in his throat. How could he tell her that he was terrified of losing her? How could he explain that his fear of disappearing, of becoming nothing, was paralyzing him? He was afraid that the closer he got to her, the more painful it would be when he eventually faded away.

"I'm fine," he muttered, his voice unconvincing.

Maya wasn't fooled. She stepped inside, her gaze searching his face for answers. "You're not fine," she said gently. "You're pulling away from me. Why?"

Aarav took a deep breath, feeling the weight of his fear pressing down on him. "I don't want to hurt you," he admitted, his voice barely above a whisper. "The closer we get, the more I'm afraid that I'll disappear, and I'll hurt you when I'm gone."

Maya frowned, her brow furrowing in confusion. "Aarav, you're not going anywhere. Why would you think that?"

"Because everything fades," Aarav said, his voice trembling. "People, memories, love—it all disappears eventually. I'm afraid that I'll be forgotten, that I'll be nothing more than a ghost."

Maya's heart ached at his words. She reached out to touch his hand, but he pulled away, the fear in his eyes stark and real. "You're not a ghost, Aarav," she said softly. "You're here, with me, right now. That's all that matters."

But Aarav couldn't shake the feeling that he was slipping away, that no matter how hard he tried to hold on, he was destined to become nothing. He looked at Maya, the one bright spot in his world, and realized that he couldn't bear the thought of her being hurt when he inevitably disappeared. He needed to protect her, even if it meant pushing her away.

"I can't do this anymore," Aarav said, his voice breaking. "I can't keep pretending that everything is okay."

Maya's eyes filled with tears, but she didn't back down. "Aarav, we can face this together. You don't have to go through this alone."

But Aarav was already retreating into himself. He couldn't risk dragging her down into the void with him. Without another word, he turned and walked away, leaving Maya standing in the doorway, heartbroken and confused.

EXISTENTIAL DREAM SEQUENCE

That night, Aarav lay in bed, staring at the ceiling, his mind racing with thoughts of his own insignificance. Sleep eluded him, and when he finally drifted off, it was not into peaceful rest, but into a vivid, surreal dream that felt all too real.

In the dream, Aarav found himself walking through a grey, featureless landscape. The sky was a dull, overcast expanse with no sun or stars to guide him. The world around him was empty, lifeless, a reflection of the void he feared. The ground beneath his feet crumbled with each step, as though the earth itself was disintegrating, and he realized with growing horror that his own body was fading. He looked down at his hands, only to see that they were becoming translucent, barely visible against the grey backdrop.

As he walked, shadows of people passed by—faceless figures who moved without purpose, their outlines blurry and indistinct. Aarav tried to call out to them, to reach for them, but they didn't notice him. He was invisible, a ghost in a world that had forgotten him. Panic surged within him as he waved his arms, shouted, and screamed, but no one turned. It was as if he didn't exist.

The landscape stretched on endlessly, barren and colorless. There were no landmarks, no signs of life. Only the endless grey and the eerie silence that seemed to press in on him from all sides. He wandered for what felt like hours, maybe days—time had lost all meaning in this empty world.

And then, in the distance, he saw it: a single figure, vibrant and full of life, standing amidst the bleakness. It was Maya. Her image was the only thing in color, a bright contrast against the dullness that surrounded her. She was calling out to him, her voice faint but clear.

"Aarav!" she called, her arms outstretched toward him.

He tried to run toward her, but his legs felt heavy, as though they were sinking into the ground. His body continued to fade, growing more and more translucent with each passing second. Desperation clawed at him as he struggled to reach her, but the distance between them seemed to grow, no matter how hard he tried.

"Maya!" he shouted, his voice hoarse with fear. "Don't forget me! Please, don't forget me!"

But Maya's image began to blur, her vibrant colors dimming as the grey world consumed her as well. Aarav fell to his knees, his body now barely visible, and watched helplessly as the last connection to his existence—Maya—slipped away, leaving him alone in the colorless void.

AARAV WOKE WITH A START, his body drenched in sweat, his heart pounding in his chest. The dream had felt so real, so visceral, and the fear of being forgotten, of fading away, clung to him like a dark cloud. He sat up in bed, running a hand through his damp hair, trying to steady his breathing.

The dream had shaken him to his core, bringing all his fears to the surface. It was a stark reminder of the thing he feared most: being erased from existence, with no one to remember him. But more than that, it was a reminder that he was pushing away the one person who still saw him, who still cared.

CONCLUSION OF ACT 3:

The crisis in Aarav and Maya's relationship comes to a head as Aarav withdraws, consumed by his existential phobia. The vivid dream sequence serves as a symbolic representation of his deepest fear—being forgotten and fading into nothingness, while Maya remains his last connection to existence. This act ends with Aarav waking from the dream, shaken and realizing the consequences of his withdrawal, but unsure of how to move forward.

Act 4: The Revelation

THE FOG OF CONFUSION that had hung over Maya's heart for weeks finally began to clear. As much as Aarav had tried to mask it, she had seen the signs of his withdrawal—his avoidance of her calls, his absence from their usual meeting spots, the way his eyes seemed to look past her when they were together. It hurt her deeply, but Maya knew that something far larger than their relationship was gnawing at Aarav. His fear of non-existence had manifested in ways she couldn't fully understand at first, but after their last conversation, it became painfully clear.

It wasn't that Aarav didn't love her—he did, intensely. But his love was tangled with the shadow of his existential phobia, a fear so overwhelming that it was choking the life out of him. Aarav wasn't just afraid of death; he was terrified of fading away, of being forgotten by the world and by her. The thought that his existence might leave no lasting mark, that his presence in the universe would be erased as though it had never been, was crippling him. And, ironically, in his effort to shield her from the pain of his disappearance, he was pushing her away.

SITTING BY THE WINDOW of her small apartment, Maya watched the sunlight filter through the trees outside, casting golden patterns on the floor. She had spent hours thinking about Aarav, about his fears, and about how she could help him understand what she saw so clearly. Aarav had always been obsessed with the idea of fading into obscurity, but to Maya, he was anything but insignificant. His presence in her life had changed her in ways she hadn't anticipated. He had made her question her own ideas of existence and memory, had shown her the beauty of art and the complexity of the human soul. He was unforgettable to her.

Maya knew that Aarav needed something tangible, something to hold on to in the midst of his swirling fears. Words, she realized, had always been her way of making sense of the world, just as painting had been his. If she could find the right words—if she could show him how deeply he had impacted her, how love and memories were more enduring than he realized—then maybe, just maybe, she could pull him out of the darkness.

THAT EVENING, MAYA sat at her writing desk, a blank sheet of paper in front of her. She hesitated for a moment, unsure of how to begin. Writing a love letter seemed both too simple and too profound for what she wanted to convey. It wasn't just about love; it was about existence, about memory, about the way people leave traces of themselves in the lives they touch.

Finally, she picked up her pen and began to write.

THE LOVE LETTER

MY DEAREST AARAV,

I don't know if you'll read this, or if you'll believe what I'm about to say, but I need you to hear me.

You once told me that you were afraid of being forgotten, of disappearing into the void, and that no matter what we do, it's all temporary. I've been thinking about those words for weeks now, trying to understand your fear. And I think I finally do. But what I want you to understand, Aarav, is that you're wrong.

You may feel like a grain of sand on a vast beach, but to me, you are everything. The moments we've shared—those quiet mornings by the sea, the late-night conversations, the times when we sat in silence and just *were*—those are not fleeting. They are imprinted on my soul, and they will stay with me for as long as I live. And after that? They'll live on in the people I share them with, in the art you've created, in the love you've given me.

You are not forgotten, Aarav. You never will be. Every time I look at the sea, I see you. Every time I feel the wind on my skin, I hear your voice. You exist in the world around me, in the colors of the sunset, in the brushstrokes of your paintings, in the rhythm of the waves.

Love, Aarav, is what makes us eternal. Not in the way we think of eternity, not in an endless physical sense, but in the way that we live on in the hearts of those we love. You are part of me now, and that means you will never fade away.

I know you're afraid, and I know that fear is real. But I want you to know that you are loved, deeply and completely. And that love is what will keep you alive, in me and in the world.

Please don't push me away. Let me be part of your world, as you are part of mine. Let's create something together, something that will last, even if we don't.

Yours, always,

Maya

MAYA SAT BACK AFTER finishing the letter, her hand trembling slightly. It wasn't perfect, but it was honest. It was her truth, their truth, and she hoped that it would be enough to reach Aarav. She folded the letter carefully and slipped it into an envelope, sealing it with a quiet determination. This wasn't just a letter; it was her way of showing Aarav that he mattered, that his fear of fading into nothingness was unfounded because, to her, he was unforgettable.

THE NEXT DAY, MAYA found herself standing outside Aarav's cottage, the letter clutched in her hand. She felt a strange mixture of nerves and hope, unsure of how Aarav would respond. She knocked on the door, her heart racing in her chest. When Aarav finally opened the door, he looked tired, like he had been carrying the weight of the world on his shoulders for far too long.

"Maya," he whispered, surprised to see her.

"I have something for you," she said softly, holding out the letter. "Please read it."

Aarav hesitated for a moment before taking the envelope from her. He didn't say anything, but the look in his eyes told her that he was grateful, that despite his withdrawal, he still cared.

Maya gave him a small, encouraging smile. "I'll give you some time," she said, stepping back. "But please, don't give up on us."

LATER THAT EVENING, Aarav sat at his desk, the envelope unopened in front of him. He had been staring at it for hours, afraid of what it might contain, afraid of facing the truth that Maya had undoubtedly written inside. His fear of disappearing, of fading into nothingness, was still there, heavy and persistent, but there was something else now too—hope.

Finally, he broke the seal and unfolded the letter, his eyes scanning the words. As he read, something inside him shifted. Maya's words were like a light in the darkness, a reminder that even in the vastness of the universe, he was not insignificant. He had made an impact on her, on the world around him, and that impact would remain, even after he was gone.

Tears welled in his eyes as he reached the end of the letter. Maya was right. Love was what made them eternal, what kept them alive in the hearts and memories of others. He wasn't a ghost; he was a part of her world, and she was a part of his. And that was enough.

ILLUSTRATION CONCEPT

The visual representation of Maya's love letter is a close-up of the paper, Maya's handwriting delicate and full of emotion. Surrounding the letter, a montage of their shared moments comes to life—Aarav and Maya walking hand in hand by the sea, laughing over a shared joke, sitting together in silence as the sun sets. Each moment is vibrant, full of color, a stark contrast to the grey, featureless world of Aarav's dream. The montage represents the lasting impact of love and memory, showing that Aarav's fear of fading away is unfounded. Through Maya's love, he is anchored in the world, eternal in her heart and memories.

CONCLUSION OF ACT 4:

Through Maya's perspective, we see her deep understanding of Aarav's fears and her determination to show him that love and memory are the true keys to eternal existence. The love letter serves as a turning point, offering Aarav a lifeline in the midst of his existential crisis. With her words, Maya provides him with the reassurance that he will not be forgotten, that he is part of her life in a way that makes him eternal.

Act 5: The Climax and Resolution

THE COASTAL TOWN WAS cloaked in the soft hues of a setting sun, the sky a blend of deep oranges, purples, and pinks, reflecting off the gentle waves. Aarav sat alone by the rocks where he and Maya had first met. It was a familiar place, but one that now felt distant, as though it belonged to a version of himself that no longer existed. In the weeks since he had withdrawn from Maya, Aarav's world had grown smaller and greyer, a reflection of the desolate fear that consumed him. He hadn't touched a brush, hadn't even looked at a canvas. The once beautiful seaside, a source of inspiration for his art, now seemed hollow.

Aarav's mind was a whirlwind of thoughts. He kept going over his deepest fear—the idea that he would vanish without leaving any meaningful mark on the world. No legacy, no memory. His existence felt fleeting, and every time he thought about Maya, it hurt. He was afraid of being forgotten by the world, but more so, by her.

Suddenly, he heard footsteps behind him, the sound pulling him out of his thoughts. He turned to see Maya standing there, holding the letter he had read just hours before. Her eyes were determined, but soft. There was no anger or frustration, only a deep compassion and understanding.

"Aarav," she called out, her voice carrying the weight of both love and sadness.

He looked away, guilt rising inside him. "I'm sorry, Maya," he muttered, unable to meet her gaze. "I'm sorry for pushing you away."

Maya shook her head gently and approached him, the letter still in her hand. "Don't apologize. I understand why you did it," she said, kneeling beside him on the rocks. "But you don't have to face this fear alone."

THE CONFRONTATION

Maya unfolded the letter, her fingers trembling slightly. "I wrote this for you because I wanted you to know what you mean to me, Aarav. But I don't think you fully understand yet. So I'm going to read it to you."

Her voice was calm but filled with emotion as she began to read the words she had so carefully crafted. Aarav sat there, listening, and as each word spilled from her lips, he felt something inside him begin to break. Maya's voice was steady, unwavering, as she spoke of love, of memories, of how Aarav had left an indelible mark on her life. She reminded him that love was the one thing that could transcend time, the one thing that made existence meaningful.

As Maya read, Aarav felt the weight of his fear begin to lift. For the first time, he realized that his obsession with being remembered by the world had blinded him to the most important thing—the love he shared with Maya. He had been so consumed by the thought of being forgotten by the universe that he had forgotten the one person who mattered most.

When Maya finished reading, she gently placed the letter beside him. Silence hung in the air for a moment as Aarav struggled to find the words. His heart was pounding, and tears welled up in his eyes.

"I've been such a fool," he whispered, his voice cracking. "I thought I had to be remembered by everyone... that if I wasn't, I'd disappear. But all this time, I was pushing away the only person who makes me feel real."

Maya reached for his hand, squeezing it tightly. "You are real, Aarav. To me, you're the most real thing in the world."

AARAV'S REALIZATION

In that moment, Aarav realized that his fear had been preventing him from truly living. He had been so focused on the idea of leaving a legacy that he had forgotten to live in the present, to experience love and connection with the people closest to him. He turned to Maya, his eyes full of tears, and spoke the words he had been too afraid to admit.

"I've been scared for so long," he said softly. "Scared that if I don't leave something behind, I'll just... disappear. But now I see that I've been wrong. It's not about how the world remembers me. It's about how *you* remember me. You're my world, Maya. And if I exist in your heart, then that's enough."

Maya smiled, her own eyes shimmering with tears. "That's all I've ever wanted you to see."

For the first time in weeks, Aarav felt a sense of peace wash over him. The fear that had gripped him for so long began to fade, replaced by a deep sense of love and gratitude for the woman beside him. He knew now that existence wasn't about being remembered by the masses; it was about the love and memories shared with those who truly mattered.

THE FINAL PAINTING

The next morning, Aarav stood in front of his easel, his paintbrush trembling in his hand. For the first time in weeks, he felt the urge to create, not out of fear, but out of love. He dipped the brush into vibrant hues of red, orange, and gold, the colors of the sunrise that spilled through the window. As the paint touched the canvas, Aarav let go of his fear and allowed himself to fully embrace the moment.

He painted Maya.

Her figure emerged on the canvas, radiant and full of life, her eyes sparkling with the same warmth and love that had saved him from his darkest thoughts. Every stroke of the brush felt like a declaration, a promise that he would no longer be ruled by fear. As he painted, Aarav felt himself reconnecting with the world around him—not as a fading whisper, but as someone who was alive, who loved, and who was loved in return.

By the time he finished, the portrait of Maya stood before him, vibrant and beautiful. It wasn't just a painting; it was a symbol of everything he had learned. Maya had shown him that love was what gave life meaning, that through their shared moments, their connection, he would never truly fade away.

THAT EVENING, AARAV invited Maya to his studio. When she arrived, he stood by the easel, the completed painting draped in a cloth. He looked at her, his eyes filled with a newfound light.

"I painted something," he said, his voice soft but steady. "Something for you."

Maya smiled as Aarav pulled the cloth away, revealing the vibrant portrait. Her breath caught in her throat as she looked at the painting, tears filling her eyes. It was her, as he saw her—full of life, full of love, the anchor to his existence.

"Oh, Aarav," she whispered, stepping forward to touch the canvas. "It's beautiful."

Aarav smiled, his heart swelling with love. "You showed me that love is what makes us eternal. And this... this is how I'll remember you. How I'll remember us."

ILLUSTRATION CONCEPT

The final illustration is a vibrant and emotional scene. Aarav and Maya stand in front of the completed painting, embracing each other with deep affection. The painting itself captures Maya in all her beauty, her image glowing with the warmth and love that has saved Aarav from his fears. The colors in the painting are rich and full of life, a stark contrast to the greys of Aarav's previous dream sequences. The scene is one of resolution, of hope, and of the triumph of love over fear. Aarav has found his place in the world, not through being remembered by the masses, but through his love for Maya, which has anchored him to existence in the most meaningful way.

CONCLUSION OF ACT 5:

The climax of Fading Echoes culminates in Aarav's emotional realization that love is what gives life its meaning. His existential fear of fading away is confronted and ultimately dispelled through Maya's unwavering support and the power of their connection. The final painting of Maya symbolizes Aarav's acceptance of love as a means of existence, and the embrace between them marks the resolution of their journey. Through love, Aarav has found peace, and the story closes on a note of hope, as Aarav and Maya move forward together, secure in their shared existence.

Act 6: The Healing Journey

AFTER THE HEARTFELT confrontation, the weight that Aarav had carried for so long seemed lighter, but he knew there was more to his fear than the immediate threat of being forgotten. It wasn't just about existence in the present or future—it was the echoes of his past, a collection of moments that had shaped his internal fear of being unseen, unworthy of love, and ultimately, of disappearing into obscurity.

AARAV'S SELF-DISCOVERY

The days following the emotional resolution with Maya were quiet but contemplative. Aarav found himself thinking about his childhood, his early days as an artist, and the struggles he had buried deep inside. These memories were sharp and often painful, but now, with Maya by his side, he felt a strange desire to revisit them. He realized that his fear of fading away was tied to his history, to moments when he had felt invisible and forgotten. Maybe, by confronting these memories, he could begin to heal.

Maya, always intuitive, suggested they take a journey together—both a literal road trip and an emotional one. "We need to go back," she said gently one evening as they sat by the sea. "To the places where you first felt lost, where those feelings of insignificance began. Let's visit those memories together and rewrite them."

Aarav hesitated, fear clawing at his chest again, but something about Maya's presence made him feel braver. She had been the anchor he needed, and now she was offering him the chance to reclaim his past, to stop running from it. With her, he believed he could face it.

THE JOURNEY BEGINS

They set out early one morning, the mist still hanging low over the coastal town as they packed the car for their trip. The road stretched ahead of them like an uncharted path, winding through valleys and across open plains. Their destination: the significant places from Aarav's past, the ones that had left the deepest imprints on his soul.

The first stop was his childhood home. The house, once filled with the scent of his mother's cooking and the sound of his father's laughter, now stood in disrepair. The windows were cracked, the paint peeling, and the garden overgrown. Aarav stood before the dilapidated house, memories flooding his mind—of painting in the small backyard, of being praised for his talent, but also of the times he had felt like a ghost, unseen by his family during their moments of turmoil.

Maya stood beside him, her hand in his, silent but supportive. She knew this was a moment for Aarav to process on his own, but her presence gave him strength. He walked up to the front porch, running his fingers along the worn wood. The place that had once felt like a sanctuary now seemed distant, but as Aarav breathed in the crisp air, he realized something important: the house no longer held power over him. The memories it contained were a part of him, but they didn't define him.

As they left, the sun broke through the overcast sky, casting a soft light over the house. Aarav looked back one last time, not with fear or sadness, but with acceptance.

MAYA'S SUPPORT

Throughout the journey, Maya remained a constant source of strength. She listened as Aarav opened up about his fears—how he had always felt like an outsider, even in the art world, how he had struggled to make a name for himself, and how the fear of being forgotten had started to consume him even in his youth. As they traveled through the city where Aarav had once tried to establish himself as an artist, he recounted the frustration of being overlooked, his work barely noticed by critics and collectors.

Maya, in turn, shared her own struggles. "You're not the only one who's felt like that, Aarav," she told him one evening as they sat on the balcony of a small inn, watching the stars above them. "I've felt it too—the fear of insignificance. Of pouring yourself into something—writing, in my case—only to wonder if anyone will care. If anyone will even remember. But what I've learned is that our worth isn't defined by the world. It's in the love we share, the moments we create, the connections we make. That's what keeps us alive."

Aarav listened, realizing how deeply connected they were by these shared fears. It was a revelation—he wasn't alone in his struggle. Maya had faced the same demons, and yet, she had found her own way to cope. Their bond deepened with each conversation, each shared moment of vulnerability.

AARAV'S BREAKTHROUGH

Their final destination was a serene mountain retreat—a place Aarav had once visited as a child, long before his existential fears had taken root. The towering cliffs and rolling hills, the sound of wind whistling through the trees, brought him a sense of peace he hadn't felt in years. Maya had suggested the retreat as a place for them to reflect, but it was more than that—it was the place where Aarav would find his breakthrough.

On the second morning at the retreat, Aarav woke with a clear vision. He grabbed his brushes, paints, and a canvas and headed to the cliffs overlooking the valley. The view was breathtaking, but instead of painting the landscape, Aarav decided to paint something far more personal—his journey. He sketched the outlines of figures, abstract representations of his childhood, his struggles, his fears, and his love for Maya. He began filling in the colors, bright and bold, symbolizing the life he had lived, the highs and lows, the pain and joy.

Maya watched from below, her heart swelling with pride and love as she saw Aarav reclaim his art—not as a tool for others to remember him by, but as a way to express his own existence, his own truth. Each stroke of his brush was a declaration: I am here, and I matter.

The mural grew larger, a kaleidoscope of colors and shapes that told the story of a man who had faced his fears and come out stronger. When Aarav finally stepped down from the scaffold, sweat on his brow but a smile on his face, he felt lighter than he had in years. The fear that had once consumed him was still there, but it no longer held the same power. He had confronted his past, his fear of non-existence, and in doing so, he had found a new sense of peace.

THE FINAL SCENE

Aarav and Maya stood together, gazing up at the mural that now adorned the cliffside. It was vibrant, alive, a testament to Aarav's journey—his pain, his fear, but also his love and his triumph. As the sun set behind them, casting a golden glow over the valley, Aarav turned to Maya, his heart full.

"Thank you," he whispered. "For being with me through this. For helping me see that I don't need the world to remember me. As long as I have you, as long as we have these moments... that's all the existence I need."

Maya smiled, her eyes glistening with emotion. "You're here, Aarav. That's enough."

They embraced, standing before the mural that now symbolized Aarav's journey of healing. In that moment, Aarav realized that existence wasn't about being remembered by the masses. It was about love, about connection, and about the moments shared with those who mattered most.

ILLUSTRATION CONCEPT

A powerful image of Aarav standing on the scaffold, putting the final touches on the mural. The mural is a vibrant, swirling mix of colors—bold reds, blues, yellows, and greens—that capture the complexity and beauty of life. Below, Maya stands watching with a proud smile, her presence grounding and inspiring Aarav. The mural itself depicts abstract representations of Aarav's life—moments of joy, struggle, love, and self-discovery—culminating in the image of Aarav and Maya together, symbolizing the triumph of love and existence over fear.

CONCLUSION OF ACT 6:

This act marks the culmination of Aarav's internal journey, as he confronts the unresolved fears and memories from his past. Through Maya's unwavering support and their shared journey to significant places from his life, Aarav finds a deeper understanding of his fear of non-existence. The mural he paints on the cliffside symbolizes his reclamation of his existence and his acceptance of life's complexities. In the end, Aarav realizes that true existence is not about being remembered by the world but about the love and connection he shares with those who matter most.

Act 7: The Return Home

AFTER THEIR TRANSFORMATIVE journey, Aarav and Maya return to the coastal town where their story began. This time, however, Aarav is not the same man who once feared the looming specter of oblivion. As they drive along the familiar road, the mist hanging over the hills and the sun setting on the horizon, Aarav feels a sense of calm he hasn't known in years. The town, with its foggy mornings and quiet evenings, no longer feels like a place of limbo between existence and nothingness. Instead, it represents the ever-changing nature of life—the ebb and flow of time, love, and memory.

COMING FULL CIRCLE

The town appears unchanged on the surface—the same narrow streets, the same sleepy cafés, the same ocean waves rolling gently against the shore. But to Aarav, everything feels different now. He no longer views the fog as a symbol of his own insignificance or the sunsets as the inevitable end to his existence. He sees them for what they are—beautiful, fleeting moments that deserve to be cherished for their impermanence.

Walking through the streets with Maya by his side, Aarav reflects on how much he's grown. The town is a part of him, not because it will remember him, but because it's where he has lived, loved, and found himself. As they pass by the bookshop where he first met Maya, a warm smile crosses his face. This place holds meaning not because it will etch their story into history, but because it holds their shared moments, their laughter, and their love.

Aarav's New Art Series

As Aarav settles back into his life by the sea, a creative energy begins to bubble within him. His journey of self-discovery has reignited his passion for painting, but this time, it's different. He no longer paints out of fear or a need to immortalize himself in the eyes of others. Instead, he paints for the joy of it, for the beauty of expressing life as he has lived it.

His new art series reflects this transformation. Unlike his earlier works—haunting and dark, echoing his existential dread—these new paintings are vibrant, alive with color and movement. Each piece tells the story of a moment that Aarav has lived, loved, and cherished. There's a painting of the sea, bright and shimmering under the sun, symbolizing the fluidity of life. Another depicts Aarav and Maya standing before the mural he painted in the mountains, their figures intertwined in a celebration of love and connection.

Each painting is a celebration of life's impermanence and the lasting impact of love. Aarav realizes that while memories may fade over time, the moments we share with those we love are what give our lives meaning. His new series isn't about being remembered by the world but about honoring the life he's lived—full of love, struggle, and beauty.

THE EXHIBITION

With Maya's encouragement, Aarav decides to hold an art exhibition in the town—a way of sharing his journey and newfound perspective with the people around him. He had once been a mysterious figure, introverted and closed off, his art often reflecting the darkness he carried within. But now, his work is full of light, vibrancy, and joy, and he wants to share that with others.

The day of the exhibition arrives, and the gallery is filled with people. Some are old acquaintances, others are strangers, but they all come to see Aarav's new work. As they move from painting to painting, the room buzzes with quiet admiration and awe. The vibrant colors, the emotional depth, the stories behind each piece—all of it touches the viewers in a way Aarav never expected.

For Aarav, the exhibition is more than just a showcase of his art. It's a personal milestone—a symbol of his acceptance of life's impermanence and his place in the world. He no longer feels the need to be remembered by everyone; instead, he takes solace in knowing that he has lived and loved fully.

Maya watches from the sidelines, her heart swelling with pride. She sees how Aarav's art has touched the townspeople, how his vulnerability and openness have shifted their perception of him. He's no longer the reclusive artist burdened by fear. He is now a man who has embraced the beauty of life, with all its uncertainties.

AARAV'S REALIZATION and Fulfillment

As the night of the exhibition draws to a close, Aarav and Maya stand together in the center of the gallery, surrounded by his paintings. The atmosphere is one of celebration—not just of art, but of life. The room is filled with light, laughter, and the warmth of human connection. Aarav's figure, once fading and grey, is now vibrant and full of life, just like the art around him.

In that moment, Aarav realizes that he has found his place in the world—not through fame or the recognition of strangers, but through love, through Maya, and through the moments he has lived. He no longer fears being forgotten, because he understands that existence is not about being remembered by everyone, but by the ones who truly matter.

As he looks at Maya, standing beside him with her arm looped through his, he knows that his life, his love, and his art will continue to resonate, even if only in the hearts of a few. And that is more than enough.

FINAL ILLUSTRATION Concept

The final illustration captures the emotional culmination of Aarav's journey. He and Maya stand in the middle of the art gallery, surrounded by Aarav's vibrant paintings. The room is filled with light, symbolic of the hope and joy Aarav has found. The atmosphere is one of celebration—people admire the paintings, their expressions reflecting the emotional depth and beauty of Aarav's work.

Aarav's figure, once depicted as fading or shadowy in earlier scenes, is now vibrant and full of life. His posture is relaxed, his expression one of peace and contentment. Maya stands beside him, her presence a grounding force throughout his journey, her smile radiant as she watches him thrive in this moment of fulfillment. The scene symbolizes Aarav's acceptance of life's impermanence, the triumph of love, and the beauty of living fully in the present.

CONCLUSION OF ACT 7:

Aarav's return to the coastal town marks the completion of his emotional and existential journey. Through his new series of paintings and the successful art exhibition, Aarav comes to understand that existence is not about being remembered by the masses, but about the love and connections he has nurtured along the way. The act symbolizes the celebration of life's fleeting moments and the lasting power of love.

Act 8: The Catalyst of Change

—-

Though Aarav had returned from his journey with a newfound sense of peace, an undercurrent of doubt begins to surface. The joy and clarity he felt after the exhibition are now tinged with a quiet fear—that this peace is fragile, temporary, and could be easily shattered by the very uncertainties of life he thought he had accepted. The weight of this realization sits heavy on his chest, like a shadow lurking in the corners of his mind.

Maya, ever perceptive, notices the subtle shift in Aarav's demeanor. His laughter has grown softer, his contemplative silences longer. One evening, as they sit on the porch of Aarav's coastal home, watching the sun sink below the horizon, Maya gently suggests they take some time apart—not out of distance or discord, but for reflection. She believes that solitude will give Aarav the space to solidify his understanding of his fears and desires, and she trusts that their connection is strong enough to withstand any separation.

"I think it's time you look inward, truly inward," she says softly. "And maybe being alone for a little while will help you find that clarity."

Aarav is hesitant at first, afraid of losing the stability they've built together. But deep down, he knows that Maya is right. His fears, though quieter now, still linger, and he realizes that they won't simply disappear. They need to be confronted, not avoided.

AARAV'S SOLO JOURNEY

Aarav decides to embark on a solo journey to a remote monastery nestled in the mountains, a place known for its tranquillity and spiritual wisdom. The journey there is long and arduous, but Aarav welcomes the solitude. The monastery is perched on a cliffside, overlooking a valley that stretches out for miles. The wind is cold and sharp, but the air is pure and clean. As Aarav arrives, he is greeted by the serene silence of the place, a silence that feels both comforting and challenging.

At the monastery, Aarav meets a wise monk, an older man with kind eyes and a quiet demeanor. The monk doesn't speak much at first, but over time, Aarav finds himself opening up to him, sharing his fears about existence, love, and the impermanence of life. The monk listens patiently, never interrupting or offering immediate advice. Instead, he tells Aarav stories—parables about the fleeting nature of life, the impermanence of everything around us, and the importance of embracing the present moment.

One evening, as they sit on the mountainside at dawn, watching the sun rise slowly over the peaks, the monk turns to Aarav and says, "Everything fades, Aarav. The mountains, the sky, even the stars. But it's not the fading that should worry you. It's how you live in the moments before they fade that truly matters."

These words resonate deeply with Aarav, reminding him of the lesson Maya has been trying to teach him all along—that love, connection, and the present moment are what anchor us in existence. He begins to understand that his fear of fading, of being forgotten, is natural but not something that should stop him from living fully.

ILLUSTRATION CONCEPT

In this moment of quiet introspection, Aarav is depicted sitting cross-legged on a mountainside at dawn. The sky above him is a soft gradient of colors, shifting from the deep blues of the night to the warm pinks and oranges of the rising sun. Beside him sits the monk, silent and serene, his presence grounding and wise. Aarav's face is illuminated by the first light of day, a symbol of the dawning clarity and understanding that he is beginning to find within himself.

The scene is peaceful, yet profound—capturing the stillness of the moment and the quiet power of introspection. The vastness of the landscape around them symbolizes the infinite nature of existence, while the simplicity of the figures in the foreground reflects the importance of embracing the present moment, no matter how fleeting it may be.

MAYA'S LETTERS

While Aarav is away at the monastery, Maya writes him letters every day. In each letter, she expresses her thoughts, her experiences, and her reflections during their time apart. She writes about the small details of her days—how the sea looks at sunset, the books she's been reading, and the quiet moments when she thinks of him. But she also delves deeper, sharing her own fears and vulnerabilities, her thoughts on love and existence, and the strength she finds in their connection.

These letters become a lifeline for Aarav. Every evening, after a day of meditation and introspection, he sits by candlelight and reads Maya's words. Her letters bring him comfort, reminding him that even in solitude, he is not truly alone. Their love, though physically distant, continues to connect them in a way that transcends time and space.

As Aarav reads, he finds that Maya's words have a power beyond simple reassurance. They echo the lessons he's learning at the monastery, reinforcing the idea that love and connection are the key to overcoming his existential fears. The letters, filled with love, insight, and vulnerability, help Aarav realize that true connection doesn't depend on constant presence—it's something deeper, something that can withstand even the greatest of distances.

ILLUSTRATION CONCEPT

This sequence of small illustrations shows Aarav reading Maya's letters by candlelight in the quiet of the monastery. The light from the candle casts a soft glow on his face, reflecting the warmth and comfort he feels as he reads her words. Around him, Maya's letters are scattered, forming a circle that symbolizes the unbroken bond between them, even though they are physically apart. In one illustration, Aarav is shown smiling softly, his face illuminated not just by the candle but by the love and connection he feels through Maya's words. The letters, each one a reminder of their love, create a sense of continuity and reassurance in Aarav's journey.

AARAV'S INNER TRANSFORMATION

With each passing day, Aarav finds himself growing more at peace with the impermanence of life. The solitude, the teachings of the monk, and the letters from Maya all work together to help him confront his deepest fears. He begins to understand that life, love, and existence are not about permanence, but about embracing the fleeting beauty of each moment.

As his time at the monastery comes to an end, Aarav feels a quiet strength within himself—a strength that comes not from the absence of fear, but from the acceptance of it. He no longer seeks to control or avoid the inevitable fading of life. Instead, he chooses to live fully, with love and intention, knowing that it is in these moments that he truly exists.

CONCLUSION OF ACT 8

Aarav's solo journey becomes the catalyst for profound inner change. Through solitude, spiritual guidance, and the unwavering connection he shares with Maya, he comes to terms with the impermanence of life. He understands that while everything fades, it is the way we live and love in the present moment that truly matters. As he prepares to leave the monastery, Aarav is no longer weighed down by the fear of being forgotten. He knows now that his existence is meaningful, not because it will be remembered by the world, but because it is cherished by those who love him.

Act 9: The Reunion

After weeks spent in solitude, reflecting on the teachings of the monk and Maya's letters, Aarav returns to the coastal town where everything began. His time at the monastery has left a lasting impact—he carries himself with a calm certainty now, his mind no longer consumed by the crippling fear of non-existence. Though the phobia of fading still lingers in the shadows of his thoughts, Aarav now embraces the idea that impermanence is not something to be feared, but something that gives life its beauty. He no longer feels the need to cling to existence through the memory of others. Instead, he finds comfort in the love he shares with Maya and the fleeting yet powerful moments that make up his life.

As he steps off the train and walks through the familiar streets of the coastal town, Aarav notices that the foggy mornings, the salty air, and the sunsets over the ocean no longer fill him with a sense of melancholy. Instead, they feel vibrant, alive—ever-changing, just as he is. The town, once a symbol of blurred lines between existence and oblivion, now represents life in all its fluid, unpredictable beauty. The fog that rolls over the horizon is not a veil hiding the truth but a reminder that every moment is a chance to exist fully.

A GRAND GESTURE

When Aarav arrives at his home, Maya greets him with a warm, knowing smile. She doesn't ask him about the journey right away, but Aarav can tell that she sees the transformation in him. There is a sense of peace between them, a quiet understanding that words are no longer necessary to express how much they mean to each other.

That evening, Maya surprises Aarav by telling him she has planned something special in his honor. Intrigued, Aarav follows her to the town's community center, where she reveals the surprise: a public reading of her new book, one that she has been working on in secret. Maya's book, she explains, is deeply personal—a love letter not only to Aarav but to life itself. The stories within the book reflect their journey together, the lessons they've learned, and the fears they've overcome. It's a testament to the power of love, memory, and the fleeting moments that make up the human experience.

The reading is held in the town's small theater, and the space is packed with people—townsfolk who have heard about Aarav's recent exhibition and Maya's work. The atmosphere is buzzing with anticipation, and Aarav feels a mixture of pride and humility as he watches Maya prepare to share their story with the world.

THE READING

The stage is simple yet elegant, with a podium for Maya and a large screen behind her displaying scenes from their shared life together. As Maya steps onto the stage, the audience falls silent, eager to hear her words. Aarav watches from the front row, his heart swelling with emotion as he takes in the sight of her, confident and radiant, ready to share the story of their journey.

Maya begins to read an excerpt from her book, her voice steady and filled with emotion. The story she shares is one of love, fear, and the acceptance of life's impermanence. She speaks of Aarav's phobia, his fear of fading into oblivion, and the way they both learned to confront that fear together. Her words flow like poetry, painting vivid pictures of the moments they've lived, the struggles they've faced, and the beauty they've found in each other.

As Maya reads, the screen behind her comes to life with images of Aarav's paintings—each one a reflection of his emotional journey. The paintings are no longer dark and somber, filled with the shadows of his fears. Instead, they are vibrant and full of life, capturing the essence of the moments he has come to cherish. The fusion of their art forms—Maya's words and Aarav's paintings—creates a powerful, emotional experience for the audience, who sit in rapt attention, captivated by the depth of their love and the wisdom of their journey.

ILLUSTRATION CONCEPT

The illustration for this moment is one of celebration and emotional depth. Aarav and Maya stand side by side on the stage, their faces illuminated by the warm glow of the lights. Maya is in the midst of reading an excerpt from her book, her expression focused and passionate, while Aarav stands beside her, watching with pride and love. The audience, seated before them, is transfixed by the words and images that unfold on the screen behind them—Aarav's paintings, larger than life, telling their story through color and emotion.

The atmosphere in the room is one of shared emotion, as the audience members' expressions range from quiet contemplation to tearful smiles. The screen behind Maya displays a rotating montage of Aarav's artwork, each piece reflecting a different part of their journey—moments of fear, moments of love, moments of clarity. The colors are rich and vibrant, a stark contrast to the grey, fading images that once consumed Aarav's mind. In this final act of collaboration, their art—both visual and literary—blends seamlessly, creating a lasting impact on everyone present.

THE AFTERMATH

When the reading concludes, the audience erupts into applause, their appreciation not just for the art but for the raw honesty and emotion Maya and Aarav have shared with them. Aarav steps onto the stage, joining Maya as they take a final bow together. It is a moment of triumph, not only for the success of the reading but for the personal journey they've both undertaken.

Later, as they walk hand in hand through the quiet streets of the town, Aarav feels a sense of completeness he's never experienced before. The existential phobia that once plagued him has not vanished entirely, but it no longer controls him. Instead, it has become a part of the larger tapestry of his life—something that gives meaning to the moments he shares with Maya, the art he creates, and the life he continues to live.

In Maya's book and his paintings, Aarav has found a way to express his existence—not as something to be feared, but as something to be celebrated, even in its impermanence. He knows now that while nothing lasts forever, the moments of connection and love are what give life its true meaning.

And in those moments, Aarav knows he will never truly fade.

CONCLUSION OF ACT 9

The reunion between Aarav and Maya marks the culmination of their shared journey—a journey that has transformed Aarav from a man consumed by the fear of non-existence into someone who has learned to embrace the beauty of impermanence. Through Maya's book and his own art, Aarav has found a way to express his deepest fears and desires, creating something lasting and meaningful. Their love, strengthened by the trials they've faced, stands as a testament to the power of connection, memory, and the shared human experience.

Together, they have discovered that existence is not defined by how long we are remembered, but by the depth of the love we share and the moments we live fully.

Act 10: The Legacy

A Collaborative Project

Following their transformative reunion, Aarav and Maya find themselves invigorated by a profound sense of creative purpose. Their journey together—marked by introspection, existential fears, and a deep connection—has reached a pivotal point where their individual expressions are ready to coalesce into a shared artistic vision. The realization that their unique talents—Maya's eloquent storytelling and Aarav's evocative visual art—can harmonize to explore complex themes ignites a fervent desire to create something enduring. Thus, they embark on a collaborative project that will become a testament to their personal and artistic growth: a book titled *Fading Echoes*.

The concept for *Fading Echoes* emerges as a philosophical exploration of existence, love, and memory. This book is not merely a fusion of prose and art; it represents a deep dive into the themes that have shaped their journey. It serves as a mirror reflecting their experiences, capturing the essence of their trials and triumphs, and offering insights into the universal themes that resonate with them. Through this project, Aarav and Maya aim to create a piece of art that transcends their personal experiences and speaks to a broader audience, celebrating the impermanence of life and the power of love.

Each chapter of *Fading Echoes* will pair Maya's thought-provoking narratives with Aarav's vivid illustrations, creating a symbiotic relationship between text and art. The narrative will weave through the philosophical questions they have grappled with, while the illustrations will provide a visual representation of these abstract concepts. This integration of their talents allows them to express complex ideas about the human experience in a manner that is both profound and accessible.

As they conceptualize the book, Aarav and Maya envision it as a tribute to their shared journey—a legacy that reflects their understanding of life's impermanence and the enduring power of love. The book becomes more than a creative endeavor; it is a symbol of their intertwined lives and a testament to their commitment to exploring and embracing the complexities of existence.

THE CREATIVE PROCESS

The creative process of bringing *Fading Echoes* to life is an intimate and transformative experience for both Aarav and Maya. They establish a studio that becomes a haven for their collaborative work—a space where their artistic and emotional connection thrives. The studio is adorned with drafts, sketches, and manuscript pages, each piece representing a milestone in their shared creative journey.

Days in the studio are filled with a harmonious blend of artistic creation and deep philosophical discussion. Aarav, deeply immersed in his work, translates the themes from Maya's writing into visual art. His paintings evolve with each brushstroke, capturing the nuances of existential questions and the emotional depth of their experiences. Maya, in turn, refines her prose, guided by the imagery and emotions evoked by Aarav's illustrations. Her writing becomes a reflection of their shared insights, deeply intertwined with the visual elements of the book.

Their creative sessions are marked by profound conversations about existence, love, and memory. These discussions not only enrich their work but also deepen their personal connection. As they explore these themes, they share their reflections and experiences, reinforcing their understanding and appreciation of each other's perspectives.

The process of creating *Fading Echoes* is not just about producing a book; it is about the journey of discovery and acceptance that they undertake together. The project becomes a manifestation of their fears, triumphs, and growth, symbolizing their shared commitment to exploring and embracing life's complexities. Through their collaborative effort, they come to understand that the act of creation is a powerful way to confront and make peace with the impermanence of life.

The book evolves into a testament to their personal growth and their relationship. It reflects their understanding that love and art are integral to confronting the existential questions that have shaped their journey. As they work side by side, Aarav and Maya find that their bond strengthens, and their creative synergy becomes a powerful expression of their shared experiences.

ILLUSTRATION CONCEPT

The illustration capturing Aarav and Maya in their studio vividly represents the collaborative spirit of their project. The scene is set in a sunlit room, where warm, golden light filters through large windows, casting a serene glow over their workspace. The walls are lined with drafts, sketches, and pages from the book, showcasing the evolution of their collaborative effort.

Aarav is depicted at his easel, absorbed in painting one of the illustrations that will accompany Maya's text. His face is a portrait of concentration and satisfaction, reflecting his immersion in the creative process. The painting in progress is a testament to his artistic vision, capturing the emotional depth and philosophical themes that Maya's writing explores.

Beside Aarav, Maya sits at a large desk cluttered with handwritten notes, drafts, and reference materials. She is deeply engaged in revising her manuscript, her face illuminated by the soft light from the window. The desk is a testament to her dedication, filled with the evidence of her meticulous work and creative energy.

The studio is a vibrant and dynamic space, filled with the fruits of their labor. Scattered pages, sketches, and completed artworks adorn the walls, symbolizing the collaborative effort that has gone into the book. In the background, a completed painting and a polished manuscript sit side by side, symbolizing the culmination of their joint efforts. The sunlight streaming into the room represents the warmth of their connection and the clarity they have achieved through their work together.

The illustration embodies the sense of harmony and purpose that defines their creative partnership. It reflects the culmination of their joint efforts and the deep bond they have forged through their collaboration.

THE LEGACY OF FADING Echoes

As Aarav and Maya near the completion of *Fading Echoes*, they reflect on the significance of their work. The book represents more than just artistic achievements; it embodies their journey through existential fears, love, and the search for meaning. It is a legacy that they hope will resonate with others, offering comfort and insight to those who grapple with similar questions.

Fading Echoes stands as a celebration of their personal growth and the strength of their bond. It represents their desire to leave a meaningful impact on the world—not through fame or recognition, but through a shared exploration of life's most profound questions. The book is a testament to their understanding that while life is fleeting, the connections we forge and the art we create can leave a lasting impact.

Their legacy is not solely in the pages of the book but in the love and understanding they have cultivated through their collaboration. They have learned that true existence is not about escaping impermanence but about embracing it fully. They find beauty in fleeting moments and celebrate the love and creativity that enrich their lives.

The final act of creating Fading Echoes symbolizes the culmination of their journey—one of acceptance, connection, and the enduring power of love. As they prepare to share their book with the world, Aarav and Maya are content in the knowledge that they have created something beautiful and meaningful. Their work reflects their shared experiences and their hope for others to find peace and inspiration in the face of life's impermanence.

In the end, Fading Echoes becomes more than just a book; it is a living testament to the power of art and love to transcend the fleeting nature of existence. Aarav and Maya's legacy is woven into every page, every illustration, and every word, reflecting their journey and their hope that others may find solace and inspiration through their shared creation.

Act 11: A New Fear

Maya's Doubts

As the completion of *Fading Echoes* draws near, a new wave of anxiety washes over Maya. The book, which has been the centerpiece of their lives for months, is almost done, and with its imminent finish, Maya finds herself wrestling with a profound sense of unease. Her fears are not just about the end of a creative project but about the potential impact on her relationship with Aarav.

Maya's existential fear revolves around the idea that their relationship, which has thrived within the context of their shared creative endeavor, might struggle once the project is completed. She worries that the intense connection and purpose they have experienced might fade as they transition back to a more ordinary routine. The depth of their bond, which has been so intricately woven into their work, feels precarious as they approach the finish line.

This new fear mirrors Aarav's earlier struggles with existential phobia but manifests differently for Maya. Her anxiety stems from the specific dynamics of their partnership, which has been deeply intertwined with their collaborative project. The sense that their relationship might lose its meaning or strength without the project as its focus creates a palpable sense of dread.

Maya's doubts are further amplified by the thought of facing an uncertain future without the creative energy that has defined their recent months. She questions whether their connection can endure beyond the scope of their work and whether their love can remain vibrant without the constant stimulation of their shared artistic pursuit.

AARAV'S SUPPORT

As Maya grapples with these fears, Aarav, who has journeyed through his own existential crisis, steps into the role of a supportive partner and guide. Having navigated his own challenges, Aarav is now in a position to offer comfort and reassurance. He recognizes the depth of Maya's concerns and approaches her fears with empathy and understanding.

Aarav takes on the role of both comforter and mentor. He shares the wisdom he has gained through his own journey of self-discovery and existential exploration. His insights are rooted in his experience of overcoming fears and embracing the impermanence of life. Aarav helps Maya understand that their relationship is not contingent upon the success of their project but is instead built on a foundation of deep connection and mutual respect.

He reassures Maya that their love and partnership are not defined by the completion of *Fading Echoes*. Instead, their bond is rooted in the shared experiences, emotions, and understanding they have cultivated over time. Aarav emphasizes that their connection transcends any single endeavor and that their relationship is resilient and enduring.

Through heartfelt conversations, Aarav helps Maya see that the strength of their bond lies in their ability to support and understand each other, regardless of external circumstances. He encourages her to trust in the depth of their relationship and to focus on the love they have nurtured, which is not dependent on any particular project or achievement.

ILLUSTRATION CONCEPT

The illustration capturing this moment of vulnerability and support is a poignant visual representation of Aarav and Maya's emotional exchange. Set in their studio, the scene is bathed in the warm, golden light of a sunset. The sky is ablaze with colors—vivid oranges, soft pinks, and deep purples—that mirror the emotional complexity of their situation.

In the foreground, Aarav and Maya are depicted in a tender embrace. Maya holds a near-finished draft of *Fading Echoes* in her hands, her gaze reflecting the weight of her fears and doubts. Aarav's arms are wrapped around her in a comforting and protective gesture. His expression is one of deep empathy and reassurance, conveying his role as a source of support.

The backdrop of the sunset adds a layer of metaphorical depth to the scene. The transition from daylight to dusk symbolizes the shift from the intensity of their creative work to the uncertainties of their future. The vibrant colors in the sky represent the enduring beauty of their connection, even as they face new challenges.

The illustration captures the essence of their moment—one of vulnerability, comfort, and mutual support. It highlights the strength of their bond and the reassurance they offer each other as they navigate the complexities of their relationship and the fears that come with change.

A NEW PERSPECTIVE

As Aarav and Maya work through this new fear, they come to a deeper understanding of their relationship and their individual strengths. The challenges they face together serve to reinforce the depth of their connection and their ability to support each other through life's uncertainties.

Maya's fear, while daunting, becomes an opportunity for growth. With Aarav's support, she learns to navigate her anxieties and embrace the changes that come with the completion of *Fading Echoes*. The experience strengthens their relationship and deepens their appreciation for one another.

In the end, Act 11: A New Fear serves as a testament to the resilience of their connection. It underscores the idea that love and partnership are not defined by the completion of a project or the absence of fear but by the ability to face challenges together and support each other through life's uncertainties.

Act 12: The Final Test

—-

A Tragic Event

As Aarav and Maya prepare for the long-awaited publication of *Fading Echoes*, a sudden and tragic turn of events shakes their world. Maya is involved in a serious accident, resulting in a coma. The timing of this event is as cruel as it is poignant, coming just as they are about to share their collaborative creation with the world. The accident not only threatens Maya's life but also casts a shadow over the future of their joint legacy.

For Aarav, this event is a profound test of his newfound strength and his belief in the enduring power of love and memory. The prospect of losing Maya, the person who has been his muse, partner, and confidante, forces him to confront the very fears he thought he had overcome. The idea of carrying on their legacy without her presence is both a daunting and heart-wrenching challenge.

In the face of this crisis, Aarav is overwhelmed by a torrent of emotions—fear, sadness, and a deep sense of vulnerability. Yet, amid the chaos and despair, he is also driven by a fierce determination to honor their shared journey and keep Maya's spirit alive.

AARAV'S VIGIL

In the sterile confines of the hospital room, Aarav takes on the role of both guardian and artist. He refuses to leave Maya's side, dedicating himself to maintaining a vigil over her. Each day, he sits beside her bed, holding vigil as he reads passages from *Fading Echoes*, hoping that his voice will reach her and remind her of their love and the life they built together.

Aarav's artistic practices become a crucial part of his coping mechanism. He sets up an easel near the window of the hospital room, creating a space that mirrors the sanctuary of their studio. The room, though clinical and impersonal, is transformed by Aarav's vibrant sketches and paintings of Maya. These artworks, filled with life and color, stand in stark contrast to the stark white of the hospital environment.

As Aarav paints, he pours all his love, fear, and hope into each stroke. His art becomes a conduit for his emotions and a way to keep Maya's presence palpable. The act of painting is both a tribute to her and a means of channeling his grief into something meaningful. The process is intensely personal and therapeutic, offering him a way to stay connected to Maya even as she lies unconscious.

Aarav's dedication is evident in the way he meticulously captures Maya's essence in his work. Each painting reflects different aspects of her—her joy, her strength, and her vulnerability. The images are vibrant and full of life, serving as a testament to the love they shared and the dreams they had for their future.

ILLUSTRATION CONCEPT

The illustration concept for this act captures the poignant and profound atmosphere of Aarav's vigil. The scene is set in Maya's hospital room, with Aarav positioned beside her bed. His easel is set up near a window, where soft, natural light streams in, casting a warm glow over the room.

Aarav is depicted with a focused yet tender expression as he works on a painting. His brush moves with a sense of urgency and care, each stroke a reflection of his emotions. The paintings on display in the room are vibrant and expressive, contrasting sharply with the sterile and muted tones of the hospital environment. These artworks are portraits of Maya, each one capturing different facets of her spirit and personality.

Maya lies in her hospital bed, her face peaceful despite her unconscious state. The room is filled with a sense of quiet determination, underscored by the presence of Aarav's art. The walls are adorned with sketches and paintings of Maya, creating a tapestry of color and emotion that brings a sense of warmth and life to the otherwise cold and clinical surroundings.

In the background, the light from the window symbolizes hope and the possibility of renewal. It casts a golden hue over the scene, representing the enduring strength of Aarav's love and his belief in the power of memory and art. The contrast between the vibrant paintings and the sterile environment highlights the resilience of their connection and Aarav's determination to keep their love alive.

FACING THE UNKNOWN

As Aarav navigates this challenging period, he is forced to confront the fragility of life and the uncertainty of the future. The ordeal tests his strength and commitment to both Maya and their shared legacy. Through his art and unwavering support, Aarav strives to honor Maya's spirit and preserve the essence of their relationship.

The experience deepens Aarav's understanding of love and memory, reinforcing his belief that these are not bound by physical presence but are instead embodied in the connections and creations they leave behind. The final test becomes a journey of reaffirmation, where Aarav learns that even in the face of profound loss and uncertainty, love and creativity can offer solace and continuity.

In this act, the power of art and love is showcased as a means of coping with existential fears and personal crises. Aarav's vigil becomes a poignant reflection of his journey, illustrating the enduring impact of their shared experiences and the strength of their bond.

Act 13: The Awakening and Resolution

Maya's Awakening

After weeks of anguish and uncertainty, Maya's condition takes a hopeful turn. One quiet morning, as the first light of dawn filters through the hospital room, Maya stirs and opens her eyes. The moment is a profound relief for Aarav, whose days have been consumed by anxiety and hope. Maya's awakening is a tentative but miraculous sign of recovery, marking the beginning of a slow but steady healing process.

As Maya gradually regains consciousness and strength, Aarav is by her side every step of the way. His presence remains a constant source of comfort and encouragement. He continues to read to her from Fading Echoes and shares his paintings, infusing their surroundings with the vibrant energy and love that characterized their time together. This steadfast support helps Maya reconnect with the world and herself, reinforcing the healing power of love and creative expression.

The experience of her recovery deepens Maya's appreciation for their relationship and the journey they have shared. It becomes clear to both Aarav and Maya that their love is not only a source of strength but also a transformative force that has the power to overcome even the most daunting challenges. Their bond emerges from this trial stronger and more resilient, a testament to the power of unwavering support and belief in each other.

PUBLICATION OF FADING Echoes

With Maya's health stabilizing, Aarav and Maya focus on the final steps of their journey together—publishing *Fading Echoes*. The book, which had been a symbol of their shared dreams and struggles, is finally ready to be introduced to the world. The release of the book becomes a poignant celebration of their recovery and their enduring love.

The publication of Fading Echoes is met with widespread acclaim. The book resonates deeply with readers, offering a raw and honest exploration of existential fears, love, and the human experience. Critics praise the seamless integration of Aarav's evocative art and Maya's profound prose, highlighting the way the book intertwines these elements to address deep philosophical themes.

Fading Echoes quickly becomes a bestseller, touching the lives of many who grapple with similar existential questions. The success of the book not only marks a professional achievement for Aarav and Maya but also validates their creative journey. They are celebrated not just for their artistic talents but also for their embodiment of resilience, hope, and love.

The book tour and launch events are a whirlwind of activity. Aarav and Maya, now partners in both life and art, are embraced by the public as symbols of strength and artistic excellence. Their story of overcoming adversity and finding beauty in life's fleeting moments captivates audiences and inspires countless individuals.

ILLUSTRATION CONCEPT

The final illustration for this act captures the triumphant and heartfelt moment of the book launch. Aarav and Maya are depicted at a bustling book signing event, surrounded by enthusiastic readers and supporters. The scene is filled with warmth and celebration, reflecting the culmination of their journey.

Aarav and Maya stand together at a table covered with copies of *Fading Echoes*. They are shown holding each other close, their faces radiating a mix of joy, relief, and gratitude. Maya's recovery and their successful book release are symbolized by their embrace—a powerful image of their shared triumph and unity.

In the background, the wall behind the signing table is adorned with a collage of images representing their journey. This includes excerpts from *Fading Echoes*, sketches and paintings by Aarav, and snapshots of the places they visited. The collage weaves together these elements to create a rich tapestry that illustrates the depth and breadth of their shared experience.

The atmosphere of the illustration is filled with vibrant colors and light, echoing the positive energy of their celebration. The room is alive with the excitement of readers and fans, reflecting the impact of their work and the enduring influence of their love and creativity. The illustration serves as a poignant reminder of their journey—from the trials they faced to their ultimate triumph, encapsulating the essence of their shared legacy.

RESOLUTION AND REFLECTION

As the book launch draws to a close, Aarav and Maya reflect on the profound impact of their journey. The challenges they faced, from existential fears to personal crises, have shaped their understanding of life and love. Their shared experience has become a beacon of hope for others, demonstrating that even in the face of uncertainty and adversity, the power of love and art can offer solace and meaning.

Their story, immortalized in *Fading Echoes*, stands as a testament to their resilience and the transformative nature of their bond. Aarav and Maya's journey has not only enriched their own lives but has also touched the hearts of many. They come to realize that their legacy is not just in the pages of the book but in the enduring connections they have forged and the love they continue to share.

As they embark on this new chapter of their lives, Aarav and Maya are filled with a sense of fulfillment and gratitude. They understand that their journey is far from over but are confident that their love and creativity will continue to guide and inspire them. With their hearts open and their spirits strengthened, they look forward to the future, ready to embrace whatever comes next with the same courage and grace that has defined their journey.